The Coincidence

GAYATRI SURYAKANTHAN

INDIA • SINGAPORE • MALAYSIA

ISBN 979-8-88909-897-3

Do you believe in coincidences? I don't.

The universe has grand plans for every one of us.

CONTENTS

PRELUDE

Pragya

Have you ever experienced magic? I have. I can touch people and figure out their entire lives. I can touch people and see through them. Something I discovered about myself when I was a teenager. The day I met Veni.

I knew I had to be with her and she was not just a friend. Veni did not understand why she was being pulled towards a certain gravity. I knew. It was her soulmate. Her soul is drawn to him every time he is around. She called it an anxiety attack and I called it a cosmic romance. We laughed at it, but I knew what she did not, and until then, I had to patiently wait. I cannot intervene.

We, Hamsaveni and Pragya, are reborn after 200 years. To save this world against all the dark forces that threaten to enter our world.

I waited forever to meet him…, I know he is waiting for me in Mayong. My other half. Who like me, has waited patiently. He has stood at the Gates of Siko dido and protected it. He no longer has to stand alone.

ABOUT THE AUTHOR

Before embarking on her writing career, Gayatri Suryakanthan completed her Degree in Visual Communication and a Degree in Journalism. She has also worked as an assistant director in a couple of Indian feature films.

PROLOGUE

Chapter 1

Mayong, a self sustained village is often feared because of its autonomy. The village Moiragaon, is next to Mayong and they share the magical powers with Mayong due to the ancestral connections. The growth in both the village is not just due to good trade it is due to the relationship they share with each other, as allies, friends and families that have been knit together for centuries with love, medicine and magic. Pragya and Hamsaveni, who are friends, the daughters of the village Doctor, also the "sarpanch", head of the village, a family that carries a legacy of magic and are healers too.

Pragya lives in the same village as her father and Hamsaveni has been married off to the neighbouring village. She practices medicine there. In the 19th century, the British have managed to capture most of India however, the could do very little to break into Arunachal Pradesh. The Adi Tribes and Bodo tribes, despite their ancient and traditional methods were able to be an independent kingdom keeping the British rule away. Many wars had been fought, many soldiers had been sacrificed. The Moirang clan was the major reason why Arunachal could never be captured despite of modern artillery and modern weapons the British had and still could not infiltrate the powerful tribes. A spy is incepted amongst the village who comes seeking recovery for his ailments and slowly the details of this powerful clan is sent to the British to break them from the inside.

The villages are under attack by the British force. Pragya and Hamsaveni are torn and they would do anything to bring peace. Their villages are raided and pillaged and they both have lost their families. Pragya and Hamsa's bloodline is doomed. They are the last of the magic clan in India. With them losing the families, it would be an end to this sect of witches and wizards in India. They decide to cast a spell to keep their bloodline intact. Pragya and Hamsa escape to the Mechung pass. They take a blood oath and cast a spell on their Rudraksha beads and hide it away in their ancient temple for their progeny to find it. Hamsa and Pragya sit down and meditate to manifest their spells. They want their progeny to meet somewhere in the next generations to keep the magic alive and continue to heal this world from its sins. They sit there in meditation till they are found and slaughtered like the others.

Present day

Ranjith

Beach always calmed my nerves. The sound of the waves washing through the shores, the air that is heavy with the sea water. Or may be it is just the sound of the water itself that gave me a sense of calm. I feel so much more at peace when near a water body. It was unexplainable. My mother used to tell me, as a kid, I happily ran Into the lake near our house and I had no fear of drowning. I stood at the pavement and looking at the morning people going about their chores, walking, jogging and just enjoying the day. I stood at the sidewalk looking at the hustle and bustle of the dawn. Taking a moment to soak in the sun which had just risen. I suddenly feel it again. The magnetic pull, the hair on my arms rose and I got goosebumps. I could smell the fragrance, sweet and musky at the same time. The world went still for a while and I was the only one who was not. I turned around and looked. The world was still. In a few seconds the brain fog cleared and I am left disoriented.

"Are you listening to me? Let's go man!" My friend Rakesh who was wearing a scowl on his face. Was yelling at me.

"What's with that face?" I ask him

"What the hell man, I have been trying to shake you out of your day dream for the last 15 minutes"

Shit…I had spaced out again. I cannot explain this to him, he would never understand. It is a complete out of body experience that I undergo frequently, like a tide that washes over me, I cannot explain It at all. I scratch my head and smile at him.

"Sorry man, kinda got lost in thoughts." He shakes his head in disbelief.

"Lets go, I wanna have a cup of tea and get home."

Rakesh was a software engineer. But his passion was gymnastics. We came to the beach every morning so he could do flips along with his team and practice. I came for the view. And the tea of course. My name is Ranjith Roy. I am a MBBS student, who wants to become an ace orthopaedic surgeon. Rakesh and I, we did our schooling together and have been friends since we were kids.

This was our routine, we came to the beach every morning, he practiced gymnastics and I watched the sea and felt the breeze on my face. Post his class, we would come to this stall and drink piping hot tea and go about our day. This was life for the last 4 years.

The hawker gave us the tea as usual and Rakesh went on about how he has to go and listen to his manager complain about his coding. I was holding the tea cup in my hand and laughing. Suddenly I felt a push and the piping hot tea spilled on my white t shirt and me. I jumped in pain and horror. I saw a group of people walking, I wanted to yell but I was more focused on the tea mark or the burn my fingers might have. But whoever it was, who spilled my tea, I wanted to give them an earful. I cussed and washed my hand with the water the tea hawker gave us.

Hamsa

I literally pushed everyone out of the way and ran in that direction. I heard a few curses on my trail. I did not care about that at all, I continued to run. I was feeling the same magnetic pull again and this time it was dragging me to its direction. I just complied. The crazed, hyper and anxious heart would beat as a fast as it could. I sometimes fear my heart would explode. I stopped awkwardly on the side walk and looked around. It was just people, walking past me, jogging and going about their day. I wiped the beads of sweat on my forehead and bent down to kneel on my knees. My friends caught up with me. My best friend gave me the look. We both silently exchanged glances and started walking silently.

My name is Hamsa. Hamsaveni. It means a swan. I am a Physiotherapist with specialisation in sport rehabilitation. My parents named me after my great great grandmother, who was a healer and I found it amusing that I, in my own way was a healer too. I sort of liked it. It somehow made me feel more powerful. My father says that after 5 generations of not having a girl child in the family, I was born to him and broke that curse. I was special and I was the apple of the eye for everyone at home. Today was a big day for me. And yet, I am at the beach today, chasing some random feeling that has been haunting me since I turned 16. I shouldn't have come to the beach. Ever since Pragya started working for the state level Gymnastics team, she would drag me here. I try to keep away from here since my anxiety attacks have become more common. It is the fear of water I think. I had never spoken about it to anyone but Pragya. She is my friend from the medical school. She was the one who initially took care of me when these episodes started. When I thought, I had some serious medical issues, Pragya told me it was deeply psychological and not physical. She might even have mentioned " Magical" but I was more rational and more of a realist.

"Veni… I am done. Let's go". My friend Pragya called out. I tuned around and looked one more time. As far as my eyes could see, I couldn't see anything that evoke this pull in me. I breath out and sigh. I close my eyes briefly and open them. I walk towards Pragya slowly.

"What time is the groom's family coming?"

Pragya looked at me with sad eyes "11 am."

"Do you really have to do this Veni?"

My parents had found a good match for me and wanted me to meet him. They even asked me if I had someone in my life. I had no one and it seemed reasonable to abide by the wishes of my parents of meeting a man of their choice.

"I am not marrying him Pragya. i am just meeting him today for the sake of my parents"

"So, if you like him, you will marry him? Right?" Pragya asked.

"May be I will." I winked at Pragya. Her face turned pale and eyes bugged out.

"No ways! I won't let you throw away years of chasing this feeling of pull. You cannot do this to me Hamsa."

Oh no…my best friend was pissed off. She calls me Hamsa only when she is angry. But to be honest, she is right. I had dragged her to the malls, restaurants, theatres and so many parking lots following this pull. I had run like a manic and she had followed. I had broken down in frustration and she had held me. Finally one day she declared, it is some cosmic connection we cannot explain. And we hadn't tried to make sense of it ever since. Pragya believed, I was having this pull to my soulmate. I had laughed at her. And have even told her she should become a romance author.

"Pragya, let's just go and meet this man…shall we?"

Ranjith

I had gotten a call from the university hospital asking me to come over for an emergency. It is not usual for resident Doctors to be called for duty however, I was different. My university and my professor's had recognised a natural talent in me. I was extremely good at diagnosis and most of the cases I had assisted were successful. I was going to be applying for being an Orthopaedic surgeon and these brownie points from my teachers were very important for me.

I was assigned to assist my professor, the case of a 19 year old boy who had multiple fractures. This boy Ashwin, was named as the next racing sensation and a whole lot of money and bets were riding on his well being. We cannot mess this up and the looks of it, his recovery was going to be extremely difficult. It would take him months and even years to walk properly. He would need a terrific Physio to help him get on his feet, leave alone that bike. My professor had recommended him to a senior physiotherapist, Mr.Vishnu Menon. I hope his team is as good as ours.

I got back home, parked my car outside the gate and got out. I rushed inside my room, took a quick shower and changed my T-shirt. This Tea stain is going to be hard to get rid of I thought. I sighed and soaked the t-shirt in a bucket of water. I locked the house and got into the car. It was cloudy and I was glad I took the car today.

I plugged in my phone into the USB and let it charge as I drove. I knew these roads like the back of my hand, 4 years of driving through the roads. I still remember the first year, when I struggled to get accustomed to living alone in a big city. I smiled to myself at that memory. My phone started to ring and I answered the call. It was one of the nurses from the hospital. She called me to tell me that our professor was already in and has gone for his routine rounds. "Shit!" I was late. I pressed the accelerator without much thought. A curve came up too soon and I suddenly I felt the pull again. I don't know if it was the adrenalin or something else. I manoeuvred the car and In the process the back tyre landed in a puddle of water. Lucky for me there was no one on the road. I literally raced against time and reached the hospital. I have to remember to thank Nurse Lucy. I quickly got out of my car and wore my Doctor's coat and ran towards the ward hoping my Professor won't see me coming in late.

Hamsa

SHIT! I stood outside the gate frozen. Shit...shit...shit!. One second I am walking out of home to get to the hospital and the next second I know, some dumbass has splattered mud all over me. I am standing outside my gate, trying to make sense of it, mentally calculating the amount of time It would take to clean up this mess. I have to be in the hospital now. Doctor Menon asked me to come see a case of a 19 year old boy with multiple fractures. He said it was very complicated and complicated was my thing. But the kind of complicated I am in right now, seems wrong. SHIT...I murmured to myself.

I took a deep breath and went to clean myself up. I texted Doctor Menon and sent him my selfie explaining my situation. He sent back a gif which said ROFL. Well at least I was safe there. I smiled to myself. I went to the bathroom and started washing my face. Doctor Menon was not only my boss, he was the coolest Physiotherapist one can ever meet. I met Dr. Menon when he had come to our college for viva. By the end of viva, I was exhausted answering his questions and I assumed he was throughly impressed. A week later, I got a call from his office to come in for an interview. I knew I would do anything to keep this job. I did everything in my power to make sure I became an ace Physio. 3 years of grinding my rear at work, I can proudly say, I was Vishnu Menon's go to gal when it came to Rehab.

I called Pragya and told her I won't be coming in today and will only get ready to meet the boy's family. I went back in and my parents were in shock looking at me.

"What happened Veni?" My mom ran towards me. She probably thought I fell down and hurt myself.

"I stepped out of the gate and some idiot splashed mud on me and drove away". Although disappointed at my state, my mom was relived I was alright.

"This is why I asked you not to go to work today." She thought for a moment… "Now go, get fresh. The groom's family will be here before noon."

By 11.30 am, the entire groom's family was in our living room. It was sort of fun to watch the family. They were lively, interactive and even oddly comforting, I must say. It was not the typical meet the bride session. It was more like a group of friends meeting each other. I just laughed at the scenario when I walked out of my room and down the staircase. It seemed like a mad house. And the families were so busy chatting up, except for the groom no one noticed my entry. Our eyes met, he smiled and my… did he have deep dimples. I smiled back at him.

"Hi…I am Krishna" he stretched out his hand to shake mine. I was a little lost in his serene face and had to practically remove my eyes and look at his hand and force my brain into coherence.

I smiled again…holding his hand and shaking it.

"Hamsaveni"

"Wow…that's a beautiful name…."

We stood there looking at each other and not speaking when we heard a throat clear. That was my dad. The family was introduced to me by Krishna. The conversation flowed freely and it was surreal. It seemed like we had known each other for a while. We lost track of time talking about my Practice, Krishna told me he was a CA and his practice. And the entire family made fun of both of us for still practicing and not actually working. We both rolled eyes and decided to take a walk in the front yard. And yet again, the entire family made hooting sounds. I felt my parents and his parents actually liked each other more than we did. When we finally got out…I felt I could breath.

"Looks like our families get along" Krishna said and I laughed. It was like he was reading my mind.

"I was about to say that…" we walked in comfortable silence. Speaking about why we chose doing what we do, our favourite books, Films, Places we've been to, friends. Without realising, it was almost lunch time. My stomach made a huge gurgling noise. We both were stunned into silence for a few seconds and broke out laughing.

"I think we should go inside and get going…" Krishna asked turning towards the house. I turned and looked back and saw a rowdy group of older people just enjoying each other's company and nodded.

We walked back together inside. Krishna called out to his family. He whispered something in his mother's ears and she smiled and nodded. She told my mother they will take their leave now and will call them in the evening. My family said adieu's to Krishna's family and they all left. The house was finally quiet again. I was surprised how well it turned out to be. How easy all of this was. It seemed too good to be true. I looked at my mother. She smiled knowingly.

"Did you see his dimples?" She elbowed me. I laughed at her silly behaviour.

"Did you see me fall into those ma...." And we both laughed knowingly. Who knew it would be so easy? Pragya was going to flip out If I told her this.

I had to go to the clinic post-lunch. I quickly had lunch and got ready to leave. I told my mother I would be back for dinner. I still felt a little dizzy after meeting Krishna. My teenage was dedicated towards bettering my education and it never occurred to me to focus elsewhere.

I took out my scooter this time. I covered my face with my dupatta and wore my helmet and started towards the clinic. I was wondering what was happening at the Hospital and mentally reminded myself to check with Doctor Vishnu about the case. Something felt a little odd. There was an empty intersection near my house that is usually secluded. I saw 2 autos standing there and was a bike which was lying on the ground and 4-5 boys of my age. One of them saw me coming and alerted the others and they started to flee. I understood something wasn't right. As I approached they took the autos and drove away fast and I saw two youngsters on the road who were bruised and battered. I stopped my scooter and let it fall and ran towards the boys. One of them was conscious and wincing in pain. One was unconscious. I had to think fast. I saw an auto approaching and ran to stop him. Told him I was a Doctor and need to take these boys to the hospital. I helped the boys up, put them in the auto. One of the boys who was conscious held the other one. I asked the auto driver to take them to the nearest hospital which was 500 meters from here. I picked up their mobiles and wallets and followed them to the hospital. The hospital emergency took them in before I could park my scooter and go inside. I went to the reception and told them it was not an accident and the boys were beaten up. Gave them the auto number in case the police arrive and ask questions.

I filled up the application form and paid the deposit amount. Luckily I had the wallets with the ID cards to write the names. The phones were locked so I could not make any call. I went in to see the boys. They were resting. Both of them were stable and the Doctors were treating them. I got a call from my clinic reminding me of my appointments today. Shit…I totally lost track of time. One of the boys phone started ringing and I immediately picked up hoping it was his family.

"Dude, where are you…?" There was a worry in the voice.

"Dude is injured and has been admitted in a hospital…" I said irritated.

"What… who are you?"

"Listen, your friends were injured and lying on the road. I have admitted them in J P Nursing home. Inform their family. I am getting late for work. I am leaving their purse, mobile in the front office. Please collect it."

I disconnected the call before the other person could respond. I instructed the nurse to hand over the belongings and told her their family is going to reach the hospital soon. I rushed towards the Clinic in panic. I was an hour late for my appointments. I cannot believe the day I had today. Life is stranger than Fiction.

Ranjith

I was in the middle of the diagnosis when Rakesh kept calling me and I couldn't pick his call. I got out and called him as soon as I could and I heard a woman's voice on the other side. She said he has been admitted in the hospital. I ran as fast as I could, jumping two steps at a time, down the staircase and got into the parking lot. I called a few other friends and told them what I heard. My heart was beating so fast, it would have jumped out of my chest. I had no idea what happened to him. How did he get into this. Is he alright. So many things ran in my mind. I will have to go to the hospital and asses the situation and then call uncle. I calmed myself and called the hospital to find out what happened.

The phone rang, the receptionist told me Rakesh was unconscious and Pradeep was conscious but still hurt. I did not understand what was Rakesh doing with Pradeep at this time of the day. Pradeep was Rakesh's team mate from the gymnastics club. I reached the hospital and rushed to the ward. Rakesh was sedated and in deep slumber. He was not in any danger is what the Doctor told me. But he had a fractured wrist, a torn tendon. Which meant no gymnastics till he recovers. Deebak was equally battered. No fractures but the boy had a swollen eye and bruises on the ribs. He could barely talk. My blood was simmering with rage. I could not fathom why would someone do this. There has to be a personal vendetta. I walked to the reception and asked them who brought them here. The receptionist told me it was a girl. She admitted Rakesh and Deebak and paid the admission fees. I was surprised. A complete stranger paid admission fees for two complete strangers. Why would someone do that unless they were the one who made this happen in the first place. I couldn't make a thing out of this bizarre information. I turned to walk but the other receptionist called me and gave me a piece of paper. I took it from her and opened it. It seemed like a vehicle registration number. The Receptionist said in a quiet voice…

"Sir, we got information that your friends were beaten up. The lady who admitted your friends told us. This was the auto number she wrote down and gave us in case they want to press charges…"

She looked at me with pleading eyes to not involve police. I had made my mind not to. I wanted to deal with these people myself.

"Thank you… the lady who admitted my friends…did she leave a phone number, address…anything?

"No sir."

Strange… why would someone do this for complete strangers.

"She made the payment right?, do you have the card number and other details?"

"No sir, She paid Rs.5000 in cash. She got a call and told us the patients family will be here and asked me to hand over the belongings to them.

The receptionist handed over the belongings to me. I was utterly confused about this person and also extremely thankful to god for sending this guardian angel in disguise to watch over my friend. However, something wasn't sitting right with me. No-one, absolutely no one would do this for anyone. The skeptical me was already doubting this mysterious girl. The more trusting side of me was thankful for this person, whoever she was. I sat down at the waiting area and gathered by bearings and called Rakesh's father.

Hamsa

A week had past since Krishna and his family met us. Apparently, Krishna's family had called my parents the same evening and told them they want the engagement to be as soon as possible.

"They are asking if we can get the engagement done before the month of December…"

My mother, as if hearing my thoughts…spoke walking towards me. I looked up and sighed.

"Amma, we just met… I would like to meet him 2-3 more and then we can decide, right?"

My mom sat down on the dining table with me.

"See Hamsa, you like this boy. He seems nice. We did a background check… they are a good family. No nonsense. It is no secret we all get along well. Get engaged and then get to know him. You will have time before tying the knot."

My mother looked at me. She was right. I liked the boy, the boy liked me, the families liked each other. I thought about it and told her

"Whatever you say mom.."

My mom gave me a brilliant smile and clapped her hands. Sometimes I wonder if she was always this silly or with age she has become more girl-friend material. I laughed at her enthusiasm.

"Ok.. I'll call Lakshmi and ask them to fix a date for engagement."

"Lakshmi?"

"Your mother in law dear."

"You are calling my mother-in-law by her name?, amma...what are you not telling me...?"

I asked my mother with a stern voice. My father walked in just then. He pulled the dining table chair and sat down.

"Your mom met Lakshmi at a kitty party. They both became friends. They learnt they have children who are of marriageable age and plotted this whole meet the bride..."

My jaw hit the ground... I looked at mom who gave me puppy dog eyes. I couldn't believe she did not tell me this. No wonder they were so chatty in the first meeting. I looked at dad

"And you knew about this?"

My dad gave me a shrug. I faked mock anger and got up dramatically from my chair. I stood there looking at them as they waited for my answer. I looked them straight in the eye

"Good choice." and I walked away.

I heard both my parents Chuckle and saying "told you so" to each other. I laughed as I walked away. I went into my room and dropped my books and notes on my study table and picked up my phone, that I had kept on charge. I had a few emails from the clinic about the next critical appointments. Especially the racer boy's case. I heard he had been operated and will be coming to rehab soon. I discussed with Doctor Vishnu about him. It was not going to be easy. Doctor Vishnu told me about his friend Dr. Deebak who was operating this case. He was the most sought after orthopaedic surgeon in the India, with a specialisation in minimally invasive surgery that was most suited for athletes and sports people. But post surgery recovery was going to be a "bitch" according to him. I laughed at the memory of him saying this.

"Hans… the boy has complicated fractures and he wants to race in the next season, which is in less than a year…can you believe the kids these days…?"

Doctor Vishnu called me Hans. He was exhausted with this patient and how he wanted to focus on getting on the bike again, not focussing on recovery, strengthening… like that did not matter. I understood his frustration and that's why I had offered to take up the sessions. I met this kid once and I knew what cheesed off Doctor Vishnu. Thankfully, it did not faze me and seemed liked this kid will listen to me. So, the email I had got was from his surgeon's office after his surgery review. Dr. Deebak's office had sent me the details of his report. The email also mentioned that Assisting surgeon Dr. Ranjith Roy will be following up on his progress with us. I closed the email and opened WhatsApp to find a few texts from Pragya, she was extremely disappointed when I told her about meeting Krishna.

"But you said you won't get married…" she sounded almost pleading. I could only laugh. She was so invested in this theory of her's that she couldn't see beyond. She sent me a few pictures from our mall outings, she had Documented all the times I was crazed and ran around. I sent an LOL back. She was busy with her patients and I haven't seen her in a while. I missed my friend and made a sad face as I looked at my mobile. But then, there was a text from an unknown number. I opened it to find it was Krishna. He asked me to save this number and asked me if he could call me. I smiled to myself and saved the number and hit the call button. I thought the week just got better.

Ranjith

It had been a week since Rakesh's accident. That's what we were calling it. Rakesh woke up a few minutes after I called his dad. He forbid me from telling him about gymnastics practice. So instead, we told him he met with an accident while coming back from work. His parents were shocked and grateful to god that their child was alive. I was still not completely convinced as to why Rakesh would lie about this incident. He has promised to come out clean after he recovers. Deebak was sent off by Rakesh and was instructed to not come back to see him till he gets out of the hospital. It was all very confusing.

I had asked my Prof. Doctor Deebak for a physiotherapist suggestion while we went to meet Ashwin and check for his weekly progress. Dr. Deebak and Dr. Vishnu were chatting up. I walked upto him and greeted him. I asked him about Ashwin's Physical therapy. He seemed frustrated with how he just wanted to get on that bike again and not worrying about the long term implications of such callousness. I agreed. Recovery was the most important aspect post- surgery.

"Anyways, I asked Hans to handle it." Dr. Vishnu said.

"What a Physio, man… I have never seen such magical hands. I swear. All my patients refer to Hans as Magician"

They both laughed. I knew I had to meet this magician and get his help for Rakesh.

"Where is the Magician btw? Doesn't Ashwin have his Session today?" Dr. Deebak asked.

"Even a magician cannot escape fate. You know… wedding bells". Doctor Vishnu mentioned.

"Good...good. Tell Hans I appreciate the sessions. The magical touch keeps getting better." With that we walked out of the hospital. I followed Dr. Deebak. Too curious to ask but I did not want to seem unprofessional.

"Sir, if you remember I had asked for a suggestion for my friend. Do you think Dr. Hans will be able to help him?" I asked Doctor Deebak. He thought for a while, and said Hans wouldn't have the time, all my patients are handled by their clinic and now Ashwin must be keeping them busy. I'll send you another good recommendation."

I was disappointed. I very badly wanted the magician for Rakesh. I nodded and followed the words of my prof.

"Ranjith, please send the weekly assessment report to Vishnu's clinic." Dr. Deebak said to me as I turned to walk out of his cabin. I nodded in affirmation and turned to walk out.

I had gotten details on the auto number in the meantime. It belonged to a guy who stayed near the Pattinapakkam beach. These guys were also a part of the gang that regularly came to the gymnastics practice. But what pushed them to do this to Rakesh and Deebak was beyond me. I will be meeting Rakesh today in a couple of hours and demanding explanation from him. He better open his mouth and tell me the truth.

I checked my email and had gotten a response from Doctor Vishnu's clinic with an update on Ashwin's PT. He was making a slow progress and yet it seemed like he was on a right track. I let out a breath and realised I have to go and meet Rakesh.

My life was very simple. My parents lived in Calcutta. I came here to study medicine and this became my home.

Initially it was a struggle to get to communicate to people but, over a period of time I fell in love with this place and it has become home now. The whole lot of my teenage, running in the streets of Calcutta, eating Jhalmoori passed through my memory and I felt homesick for a bit. Just then, I passed a small chat shop and decided to get a bite. Something close to home. At least a taste. I parked my bike, got down and walked into the restaurant.

I went to the parcel counter and placed my order. I called Rakesh and asked him if he wants something to eat. He asked for a coke bottle alone. I laughed and waited for my order to be called out. Rakesh was one reason why I chose to do my medicine here in Chennai. We did our schooling in Kendriya Vidyalaya and after his dad got posted out of Calcutta, he settled here in Chennai. We never lost touch. And when it came to choosing a medical college, Chennai was my obvious choice. My father's demise during the first year, mom's accident and death in the 3rd year had been all bearable only because of Rakesh and his family. So when someone has hurt my best friend and I don't know why, the rage only kept consuming me.

A bell rang and the waiter called out for jhaal moori. I walked up to the counter. Before I could reach for the order, someone else picked up the parcel. I was slightly taken aback.

"Excuse me! I think that is my order" I said.

The man turned to me and said

"No man! I ordered it first…yours will be ready in a bit I think."

Strange. In so many years of ordering from here, I've never met anyone who has ordered jhaal moori. I nodded at the man. He walked a few steps and stopped and turned back. He walked towards me again.

"I am sorry to bother you. But are you a Bengali?"

"It is alright. I grew up in Calcutta…"

"Oh… Hi! I am Krishna Kumar."

"Nice to meet you Krishna..I am Ranjith"

"So, since you grew up in Calcutta, I assume you speak Bengali?"

I nodded at him. He smiled enthusiastically.

"Great…can you tell me how to say I like you…in Bengali.?"

"Are you proposing? Cos its different for different relationships…"

"Not really…but I like her and want to express that in her mother tongue"

"Ami tomakey bhalo bhaashi.."

He repeated it and kept saying it… I smiled at him walk away waving at me and trying to keep repeating the words. I laughed looking at him.

The waiter called out for my order making me jump in my tracks from the mental trip I took to love land of other people. I picked up the order and drove towards Rakesh's house.

I parked my bike outside Rakesh's house and took the parcel along with me. I saw a pair of slippers outside his house. When I went inside there was a girl in Rakesh's room. A physio. She was giving him some exercises. But there seemed to be much more undercurrent than what he was telling me. He looked at me and smiled a little. The session finished soon.

I introduced myself to the Physio.

"Hi..I am Doctor Ranjith Roy…"

"Hello Doctor I am Pragya."

We shook our hands. Rakesh told me she was the team physio for his gymnastics team. I asked her if Rakesh will be Able to compete in the championship this year. She gave me a sad smile and said, it is important we focus on recovery for now. Rakesh was disappointed but he agreed nonetheless.

Pragya seemed like a nice person. I offered her some Jhaal moori. She thought for a second and laughed.

"I know only one other person who eats this." Pragya said. I looked up at her with surprised eyes and mouthful of jhaal moori.

"My friend Veni. She is mad about this." And shook her head in disbelief. Rakesh smiled knowingly. I looked between the both of them and continued to eat my snacks in silence.

After Pragya left, I looked at Rakesh with questioning eyes.

"Ok, I'll explain."

I sat upright to listen to him.

"Pragya is my schoolmate. We were friends for a very long time. Probably the only friend after you I stayed in touch with."

I kept looking at him in disbelief.

"She is a physio. Got busy in her practice and we lost touch. School reunion poirnthen. I met her there and we connected. I referred her to the gymnastics team as a physio. We had nothing going on."

"You HAD nothing going on…so? What about now?"

Rakesh swallowed and cleared his throat.

"She joined the team about 4 weeks back. A boy in the team started to hit on her and it sort of became a problem. Richard, that pattinapakkam fellow, He was after her life. Stalking her. After the practice one day; remember? Someone even spilled tea on your t-shirt? I had asked him to back off. This is a retaliation for that."

My jaw touched the floor. So much had happened and I was unaware of any of this. I felt guilty and also felt angry.

"I was right there dude. You should have told me right."

"No dude, I did not even know if she liked me. I wanted to see where it went."

I was so proud of this boy. Or should I say man. He wanted to understand what the other person felt before announcing it to the world.

"Luckily she is a physio. Easy for you guys to sneak around. Right?"

He laughed.

"I had gone and asked my Professor recommendations for the best physio, from Dr. Vishnu's clinic. And here you are, taking private lessons."

Rakesh laughed out a loud laugh.

"Machi Pargya is Vishnu's junior. FYI."

I was shocked.

"Seriously? See, we think alike"

"I was trying to get PT Hans for you. But he is too busy. Apparently ace physio. He is known as Magician"

Rakesh thought for a moment.

"Hmmm… I'll ask Pragya about him."

We sat in silence for a while. Spoke about everything else and I had to leave to go and get my stuff sorted for the coming week. I said my goodbye's to Rakesh, uncle and aunty and left for home.

This week seems like a good week.

Hamsa

The entire week passed in a blur. Meeting Krishna, Getting to know him. Falling for his dimples. His love for books. Everything seemed so magical. I couldn't stop laughing. And my jaw hurt from smiling all the time, thinking of him. We went out for movies together, I learnt his favourite song. We went to my fav. Chat joint and he tried "jhaal moori". I explained to him what it is. I told him about my Bengali grandmother. The Calcutta connection. He even learnt how to say I like you in Bengali and surprised me pleasantly. Some stranger taught him to say "I love you". I found it extremely sweet.

Work was great. In fact my racer patient was recovering faster than I had expected. His dedication and grit to get back on that bike was the only reason. I felt proud and promised him I would do everything to facilitate his recovery and progress.

I had been covering Pragya's patients for her in the last few weeks. She had been disappearing for a couple of hours. She walked in all happy to the office.

"Going on a date?"

She threw me a dirty look. I just shrugged.

"A boy from my Gymnastics class has Minor fractures. He asked for my help and I am doing it."

I eyed her and it did not seem like a help she was doing.

"What are your intentions woman.?"

Pragya laughed.

"No intentions as of now."

"As of now? Your intentions will change later?"

"OMG! Veni! I don't know. He is my classmate from school, I like him and that's all."

"Since when do you like him?"

I was shocked. How did I not notice this about Pragya. May be I was just too lost in my own world.

"Aren't you supposed to meet Krishna? You have to shop for your Betrothal right?"

Oh shit! I totally forgot that I had to meet Krishna today at Kay and get our engagement clothes. I fumbled with my phone and saw a few msgs from him.

I cringed and hit my forehead with my phone.

I picked up my bag and other belonging, kissed Pragya on the cheek and told her she is not off the hook cos of this and ran out. I called Krishna and told him I was on the way. I hope I look as good as I feel.

I reached kay in about 15 mins. 5 minutes later than I had promised. Krishna and our entire family were already inside kay.

I parked my scooter and walked into the store. My mom and Krishna's mom were busy ogling at some lehengas for themselves.

Krishna was standing near the sherwani section with his hands inside his pocket and head tilted up looking at something. The man was gorgeous and as if on cue his head turned towards me and he smiled. And I missed a step. His dimples always did a number on me. We both grinned at each other.

"Sorry, I got stuck at the clinic.."

"Its ok… come."

He took my hand and walked towards the ladies section from across my mom. I turned towards her and made a "oh my god" face. My mom retuned my enthusiasm. And we laughed silly from across the room.

After looking at clothes for almost a few hours, we decided green for me and beige for him would be a good combination. We chose everything unanimously and that was my favourite part.

Our engagement was in 4 days. Our parents had decide the venue, made arrangements. I had invited Pragya, Doctor Menon and few other colleagues. I wanted a low key event. Krishna had invited his best friend Diya and few other colleagues. Diya was Krishna's bestie from

Kindergarten. They got each other's jokes, I even asked Krishna why hadn't they thought about getting married. Krishna just shrugged and said "I don't feel about her that way and neither does she."

Diya had a boy friend from college and Krishna was although not approving of him, was happy because she was happy.

The engagement day went as it came. The family, the hustle bustle, food, photographs, people dancing and wishing us. We all laughed at each other, with each other. It was probably the best day of my life so far.

Post the function, Krishna's mom came upto me and said she is very happy that Krishna and I found each other. She held my hands and said, Krishna is sometimes very indecisive, he doesn't know what he is doing. Please bear with him till you fully understand him. I could only smile at the gentleness with which she put across this request. The heart of a mother I thought.

Krishna walked upto me as his mother walked out smiling.

"Whats your Mother-in-law saying?"

I looked at him laughing. It was nice to hear that from him. Sort of intimate even.

"She asked me to take care of you" I said looking into his eyes.

His eyes smiled this time and I saw it glow with fondness. I think sometimes we don't need words to express. Just the way we look at each other is enough communication.

Ranjith

Losing people we love is probably the most difficult thing to explain. How empty we feel in the absence of our loved ones and how it affects us in our solitude. The constant longing on wanted to be held my mother was always there. But today, it seemed to have become unbearable. I felt my parents absence today more than ever. I stood at Rakesh's house balcony and was looking at the traffic. Aunty came up behind me with a cup of coffee in hand.

"Come, sit here" she said

I took the cup and sat at her feet. She poured some oil on my scalp and massaged it. It was probably the most relaxing time I have had in the last few weeks.

"You should do this once a week, it relaxes your body…"

With that she patted on my head and picked up her coffee. I sat there on her feet..laying my head on her lap. Feeling the care of a mother. Although not mine. But still mine in this moment.

Rakesh walked out of his room. Sat down next to me.

"MD applications are done?"

"Yeah…sort of. Professor Deebak said he will handle it."

"Nice. What happened with that girl, Amala?"

Amala was my classmate. We dated briefly for a few months. Both of us being Doctors, it never really worked out. The schedules were so messed up.

"Amala… is leaving to the USA to do her M.D… I think"

Rakesh nodded and we sat in silence. Rakesh's mom picked up our coffee mugs and left us alone.

"I am going to ask Pragya out..." and he looked me in the eye. I sort of knew he liked that girl and vice versa.

I smiled and said "all the best"

He just smiled.

"I am meeting her tomorrow near Savera. Will you drop me?"

"I'll wait and pick you up also."

"Thanks machan"

Hamsa

The wedding preparations were at peak. My work was not getting any easier anyway. I had to proof check the wedding cards and go to office and work with my patients.

I went to menaka cards and picked up a few wedding cards which were printed. We had selected 3 different designs and had a few copies of each for both the families. It was a beautiful of-white paper with golden print. One design was a traditional wedding card and one was for our friends.

I picked up everything and left the store. I put the bag inside my scooter, under the seat and got a call from Krishna. I smiled to myself and picked his call.

"Guess where am I at?" I asked

"Ummm...my home?" There was a tension in his voice that I could feel.

"Um no...just picked up the wedding cards for proof reading. Where are you?"

"I am at our wedding venue actually. I want to meet you…can you come here please?"

My heart became a puddle and mushed out.

"Of course. I am on my way. I will see you in 15 minutes ok?"

"Sure. Bye…"

Krishna has never asked me so openly to meet me like that. It was cute. It was cloudy and I suddenly was scared it would start raining. Made a mental note to take the car out from this week onwards.

My clinic was very close to the wedding hall we booked. In fact it was right across the road. I don't have to worry about parking. I can park the scooter and walk across the road and meet krishna.

I reached my clinic on time…luckily no rain. I opened the scooter's boot and took out the invitations to show krishna. And straightened my clothes and hair.

Pragya walked out of the clinic room. And was surprised to see me.

"Hey, what are you doing here?"

"Krishna said he wants to meet me, he is right across the road."

"Ok… your appointment is late. Go get your man."

I could see a bubble of laughter in her voice.

"Ok madam…as you say".

I took everything in my hands and crossed the road. I saw Krishna's car parked inside the parking lot. I walked towards it and waited. Krishna was talking to someone over the phone. So I walked away a little and stood away so that I don't look like I am eves dropping. He saw me… raised his finger to show 1 minute. I nodded in return.

Krishna kept the phone down and got out of the car. He looked as handsome as ever. He did not smile his dimpled smile like always. He gave me a half smile…

"Hey…"

"Is everything ok? You seem tensed…"

"Yes…yes everything is ok." He kept looking at the ground. His hands in his pocket. Anxious energy bubbling out of him. There was something he desperately wanted to tell me.

"Krishna…look at me." I walked closed to him.

"What happened. Just tell me."

He looked up at me. Took a breath and composed his nerves. I waited for him to speak to me. And he did.

"You know Diya… she is my best friend. And no one gets me like she does. And both of us always thought that we were just friends…but the truth is…we are more than friends and we did not realise it. We love each other. I realised it today. And I knew it would be wrong if I married you, we would both be miserable"

I felt the weight of his words. He realised he loved someone else. I realised he did not love me. I kept looking at him. Composing my mind. My logical brain took over. I nodded.

"I understand. I am glad you told me this before we got married."

"You do? You are ok with calling off the wedding?"

"I am not ok with it. But I understand what you are saying Krishna. And you will be talking to our parents and calling off the wedding."

Perhaps he thought I would create drama. I would yell and shout and create a scene. I did not. I won't stay at a place that does not value me.

He nodded and turned around to leave.

"I am sorry Hamsa, I did not mean to hurt you. I hope you know that. "

I saw a sincere guilt in his eyes. I did not say a word. He stood looking at me as if expecting me to say it was alright. It wasn't alright and I won't be giving him that answer. But I am not going to break down in front of him too. Somehow my ego became bigger than the love I had for my ex-fiancee. I stood there stubbornly, diagonally opposite to his car. Waiting for him to leave.

He sat inside his car, looked at me for a second and drove off. I felt relieved. The kind of relief you get when you breathe after holding your breath for too long. The kind of relief that you find after eating a whole day of staying hungry.

I stumbled and leaned on the car behind me to steady myself. My whole life seemed like a lie at that point. I had imagined the next 40-50 years with this man, the names of our children, how we would take care of each other. His smile, his speech his touch everything became a lie in an instant.

Before I could realise, I had started walking. I wanted to show him the wedding invitations but I guess we won't be needing them anymore. Everything slowed down around me. But I was moving. The clouds had descended and it was already windy. I knew there's going to be a downpour. I just have to cross the road and go to office.

But the 100 mts of distance seemed like 100kms. My feet wouldn't move. All the plans with Krishna breaking one by one, my eyes were filled with tears but I refused to let the tears fall.

I stepped onto the road to cross the street but something pulled me in the opposite direction. The invitations in my hand flew, a force had pulled me against the road and as I turn, I only see a face, two eyes filled with worry, and horror. His eyes locked with mine his hands holding my wrists firmly and I could count seconds before I went so close to him, I could feel his breath.

Our eyes never looking away from each other, we were both stuck in that moment. Him holding me in his arms and just then a tear decided to slip away. He did not blink. A hand came to my face and a finger wiped away the tear. I never wanted to be so close to anyone.

The magnetic pull I felt towards this man, the crazed hyper anxious heart, the hollow I felt in my chest, everything seemed to have calmed down. In one second, I forgot where I was. And then impossible feeling of staying away from him.

In that second I felt what he felt and I could tell that we were both equally lost in each other. May be this is what love feels like.

I was jousted out of the reverie. A rude shock shook both of us out of our trans. I saw Pragya's worried face. She was standing with someone who looked equally worried. He seemed oddly familiar.. he seemed to try and recognise me too.

Ranjith

She was still in my arms. Holding me so close, not wanting to let me go. I could feel her breathe. I wanted to stay here in this moment forever. Looking at her. Something stirred inside my heart when I saw her tear up. A part of me wanted to hold her so tight that her pain would melt away.

One second I was somewhere else and in the next second the world went still and I could only see her. She was dejected, even lost. If I had not snatched her at that point, she would have been hit by a speeding car. I pulled her out from the road and we stood there. Holding each other like the world existed between only the two of us.

The rain was a testament that the world celebrated us meeting under the sky today. Perhaps we had been star-crossed but today meeting her here was not a coincidence, is what my heart was telling me.

Rakesh and Pragya had come running to our side. This girl looked at the both of them and something crossed her face. She let go of me slowly… afraid that I would disappear if she did. I let go of her gently and stepped away. At that moment the air changed. As if charged with some unknown electricity and I know she felt it too cos her eyes went wide looking at me when that happened.

I had never felt this way. A connection so powerful with anyone just looking at them.

I had come here to drop Rakesh who was meeting Pragya. I should ask him about that. Pragya took this girl along with her inside the clinic. Rakesh and I stood there for a few seconds and we left.

We reached Rakesh's house, changed our soaked clothes and sat down. Rakesh seemed equally confused. Something was bothering him. I was about to ask him when my phone started to ring.

It was my meemaw… my mother's mom. I cringed, she had called me a couple of times in the last few weeks and I have not had the time to call her back.

I picked up the call. It was my uncle. He asked me to come and see meemaw and told me she doesn't have much time. I ran my hand over my face. I knew this day will come but not like this. Not when I am not prepared. I walked back into the room where Rakesh Stood. He looked at me with questioning eyes.

"Its Meemaw. She is not keeping well. They have asked me to come and see her".

Rakesh just nodded in understanding. Losing one more family member is not easy.

I looked at Rakesh and asked him

"That girl on the road… Pragya's friend! You know her?"

He shook his head in refusal.

"No…but I think she is the one who admitted me and Deebak in the hospital. I vaguely remember seeing her face."

I was surprised. I wanted to meet her and thank her for Rakesh.

"I called Pragya and asked her to confirm this from her, turns out she was the one who saved us that day."

We both smiled.

"Such a small world. Your girl friend's friend saved your life. Btw did you tell Pragya?"

"Nope..."

"We are even now...she saved your life, I saved her's... that's all."

"That's all? It looked like it has all just started, the way you held her..."

He laughed and I threw a shoe at him. But he was right. We were far from over. We have just begun. I could feel it.

I booked my tickets to Arunachal. Yes, that where my Meemaw lived. It is a gorgeous valley of nature. And there is something magical about it. I had 4 days before I left and I had to sort out my schedules with my Professor and inform him of this emergency.

I also wanted to meet this girl, what was her name, why did she seem so familiar. She had done a number on me and I couldn't stop think of her.

Hansa

I went back home and told my parents about what Krishna had said. My parents were furious and distraught. My folks called Krishna's folks. They came over and all of us spoke. Krishna came along as well.

Both the families were giving him hell. I let him get it for a while since he deserved it. But I stepped in and asked both the families to stop blaming him for being honest.

"What if he had gotten married and realised he doesn't love me? Wouldn't that be miserable for both of us and to you all seeing us miserable. Yes he is an idiot for not realising that he loved Diya...but when he did, he made the right choice. Let's stop fighting like children.

Go and just do what you guys need to do."

After I went on a rant, everyone calmed down. Krishna thanked me silently. I gave him a reassuring smile. I no longer felt the pain of disappointment that I felt when krishna told me about Diya.

All I can think of right now is that guy, who saved my life. I had to call Pragya and ask her about the guy who was with her too. He is the same guy I saved a couple of weeks back. What is he doing with Pragya. My phone range while I was thinking of all of this. It was Pragya.

"I was just thinking of calling you di"

"How are you? How are things at home?"

"Hmmm...everyone's angry, but I think we'll be fine..."

"Fine? How are they not breaking his jaw for doing this to you..."

"Calm down jakie chan...tell me something, what's the name of that boy, who was standing next to you today?"

She hesitate for a while.

"Rakesh. He is that gymnastics guy..."

"Oooooo... not bad Pragya, good choice."

"Tell me, did you admit Rakesh in the Hospital by any chance?"

"Yes! I wanted to call you. I told you the other day about two guys who got hit...this was one of them."

I could hear a commotion in the background at my house.

"Ok Pragya, I got to go. Bye"

I cut the call and walked out of my room. My mom was hysterical. She was crying and throwing tantrums. My dad was trying to calm her down. Finally she sat down and my dad hugged her to console her.

My dad was an IAS officer. He met my mother in the North east when he was posted there. They fell in love with each other and till now I see it and feel it.

I walked towards them. My dad looked at me and his eyes went soft. He loosened the grip on my mother and she also looked at me. In that instant I could remember that stranger who had held me like that.

My mother was crying. She wiped her tears. And held my hand.

"I am sorry I put you through this.."

"Ma… it was not your intention…"

"I know, but still… I know you liked him and I don't want to be a reason why you had your first heart break…"

And she started to weep again. She kept ranting how we should have gone and given our respects to her village goddess and that is why this did not work out and she broke into sobs.

I got up from my chair and went and hugged her. I knew what would make her feel better.

"Ok…I will give you a punishment. You have to accept it. Ok?"

She looked up at me suspiciously.

"Lets go and worship your Siang this year..ok?"

My dad laughed a hearty laughter. My mother was stunned. This is something she has been asking me ever since I turned 18. To come and make my offering to her village goddess and the great river of Brahmaputra as a mark of respect. I thought it would be a nice get away from all this nonsense and I wouldn't have to answer anyone.

"You are not joking right?"

"Ma… why will I joke? Let us go. I need a break too"

My mother did her silly dance and both dad and I could only laugh at her. Just like that my mom was back. Although it scared me to go to the rivers, I would do anything to keep my mother smiling.

I have to talk to Doctor Vishnu to reschedule my appointments. I am sure he would understand. I called him up and told him about the break up, the drama and how much I have to deal with. He seemed upset and asked me to take as much time off as needed and come back with the same magic touch. I laughed and thanked him. Time to book the tickets to the fairy land.

Ranjith

I reached home without much trouble. The weather is usually a problem sometimes. My Uncle was there to pick me up at the airport. It was surreal seeing him. He was the only one who remembered me as a child and held all of those memories of me. After my parents death, mama had become more of a friend and guide. He hugged me tight. The kind of hug that says everything. I yearned for that kind of love. We drove back home speaking of our good times. How the valley has changed. Meemaw's health and how she always kept saying she had to see me. I felt guilty for not turning up earlier. I should have come when she was still active. But we do not accept that our parents and grandparents will die at some point.

I walked into my uncles house. All the memories came back flooding. I had to hold onto the door as they washed over me. For a second, I was back here as a the only grandchild that the family celebrated. I was the only son to my parents. My uncle never got married. My parents had met each other while my mother had gone to finish her medicine degree in Calcutta medical college. My father, who was her senior in college, came from an Army family. It was not easy for them but the braved all odds to be with each other. I think that's love.

I walked into my meemaw's bedroom. She was short about 5ft, chubby, and fair. Like any other Hill Miri woman. She was from the Miri tribe from the hills of Arunachal. She often told me her stories of growing up. Their trials of living under the British rule and how their tribe had managed to stay autonomous for a long time. Meemaw's family were healers. A very well respected family that carried a legacy of medicine. Tribal medicine. My mother was the first Doctor in the family. I followed her foot steps. Meemaw, on the other hand was a healer. She spoke with compassion, she was kind and considerate, her words were full of Wisdom always.

"Nature is our mother" she often said. "Nature will provide for you, Nurture you, Feed you, cloth you and comfort you but, if you do anything that would upset nature, she will become a beast and destroy you. I remembered this conversation I had with her. We were sitting under the bamboo shrubs and making dinner.

All these memory of a wise woman came back flooding. My eyes filled with tears and I felt my heart try to squeeze out of my chest when I saw her lying on the bed. Half her size. Almost like a mummy. Skin like a shrivelled raisin. She turned towards me and looked at me. She had no energy. And yet her eyes twinkled a little. I went and sat next to her bad and held her tiny hand. She had lost all her teeth and only air came out when she tried to say something. She turned her head and looked at my uncle and raised her hand towards something.

My uncle understood and went and brought a book and placed it on meemaw's chest. She held the book close to her heart and ran her finger through it. She gestured me to pick up the book. I obeyed. I took the book and looked at the tattered pages. Kept it aside and looked at my meemaw.

My uncle who was sitting on the other side of the bed and held meemaw's hand looked at me.

"It's time Ranjith."

I held on to my meemaw's hand tightly. She smiled at me and ran her hands through my head and my face. This was her usual. She chanted her magic words when I was a kid and I would instantly feel better. She was doing the same thing now. She chanted holding both my and my uncles hand and blew a breath on my face. She lied back on her pillow and we could no longer see her chest rise and fall. I knew she was gone.

Hansa

It was so surreal being back to my mothers village. A quiet and quaint village in the valley of Arunachal. We would wonder if such places existed in our country. Lush green trees, clean air and water. Although the place has changed a bit. We have better roads now. My mother's parents were gone but she had her extended family who lived here. In a few days the "siang" festival would start, the entire village was getting geared up for the same.

We placed our bags in our rooms and freshened up. My cousins came up to me and asked me if I needed something. I felt so much at home here. I asked them what are the places I can see around here. I wasn't going to let go of this opportunity of vacationing. I learnt that there a few waterfalls around here, some scenic view points and hikes. Being close to water was out of question.

I asked my parents if I could go with my cousins on a hike the next day and enjoy the view. My mom was more than happy. She asked me to go and explore.

"Hansa, this place is our home and we are safe here."

I made plans with my cousins for the next day.

"We will leave at around 4 am. It is the hills so the sun comes up pretty early." My cousin Ronith told me. Ronith was an entrepreneur. He sold bamboo artifacts to the rest of the country. He had travelled the world and yet decided to stay back here and live his life.

"Hansa, do you mind if I invite a friend of mine? He has come back here after a long time. He could use this opportunity."

I thought for a second. "its fine by me Ronith. I don't mind. Everyone needs to experience thus beauty."

Ronith laughed at that "then you should come here every year and enjoy this. I would love to host my sister."

My heart was a mush "Awww...thank you Ronith. I feel so blessed."

Ronith enveloped in a warm hug.

"That's what big brothers do."

I knew that Ronith got the news of my broken marriage. And without trying to be nosy, this was his way of telling me everything will be alright. I hugged him back and let the emotion wash over me.

He pulled away from me and smiled.

"Alright then, 4 am tomorrow. Now get some sleep. I can't carry you to the mountain top."

I laughed and walked back into my room. I sighed and retired to my bed. In 2 weeks, my life has changed. In the most uncertain ways. I turned off the light and went to bed.

Ranjith

It was a week since meemaw passed away. I informed my boss that I won't be back for 3 weeks. Meemaw had lived a full life. She was loved and adored by her family and friends. The entire tribe paid respects to her. I met people I had forgotten, existed. I might have lost my grandmother to time, but I gained so many more people in her death. She did not leave me alone here. She made sure I knew I had my people.

After the rituals were over, a young man walked to me. He had kind eyes and he seemed oddly familiar.

He smiled at me and extended his hand

"Ranjith...Hope you are holding up alright."

For a second I went back to being the 10 year old boy who had come here for summer vacation and made friends.

"Ronith…is that you?" I took a step and hugged him. He smiled a hearty laughter and hugged me back.

"Listen, Ranjith… I am sorry. I did not know how to reach you when your mom and dad passed away. I am sorry you had to go through that by yourself."

I looked at his genuine expression.

"It is alright man. It was difficult. But hey, I got through." I shrugged and he patted by shoulder.

"Alright man. Hey, give me your number. I will get in touch with you after you are done with the traditions. You are here for the siang festival right?"

"Yes, yes I am. Meemaw wanted that. Here, take my number."

We exchanged the numbers, bid adieu. It still felt surreal. Me, here in a village. I belong here and felt like that. I stood there, over looking the valley from my home, if I could say that. The sun had set and the homes slowly started to turn the lights on. It felt like my life was beginning.

The traditional way of saying goodbye to my Grandmother was over. I had one more week before I went back to being an aspiring Doctor. Siang festival starts in another 2 days. I finished my dinner and was starting a fire in the backyard to keep myself warm. My phone rang. Ronith was calling me.

"Hey man, what's up?"

"Hey Ranjith. You up for a hike tomorrow?"

Wow, that's something I never thought about.

"Umm, sure, I am not doing anything tomorrow. So, sure. What time?"

"We leave at 4 am. I will come and pick you up. Well go to the Mechuka village. Watch the sunrise, drink some tea and come back."

"Sounds like a plan."

"See you tomorrow man, sleep well."

I put out the fire I was starting and went to bed. I was excited after a long time. I set my timer to 3.20 am and closed my eyes.

Hansa

The alarm started to blare at 3.15 am. It startled me from my deep sleep. "Shit" I signed and sat up straight. I am a morning person and getting out of my bed is never an issue. But the warm bed was too good to leave. I remembered, I promised Ronith I will come to the trek. I got out of my bed and got ready.

I dressed up in my yoga pants, trekking shoes and a cap to cover my ears. The weather was chilly and as I walked out of my house, a cold breeze hit my face. I heard the rumble of an engine and walked towards the gate. Ronith had got his open jeep. I closed the gate behind me and went and hopped into the massive vehicle.

"This looks Fab Ronith."

He smiled his proud smile.

"Are we ready to rock and roll?"

"Sir yes sir!" I fake saluted him.

We both laughed and drove away.

"So, my friend Ranjith is going to be joining us too. We'll pick him up and go to the Mechuka village"

"Alright. Lets go."

We drove for about 5 minutes till we reached a double storey house. It seemed ancient and traditional and something about that house drew me in. I got out of the jeep and stood in front of the house. It seemed so familiar. I have never been here and yet this felt like some place I have visited so many times. My heart lodged in my throat when a man walked out of the house and he also froze seeing me. The same guy who saved my life. I couldn't believe my eyes. Was I dreaming? My sleep deprived brain was playing tricks. That's what they say right, when you don't sleep enough, your sub conscious takes over. And you see things that matter to you or has great effect over you. And before I could get my head in place, this man was standing right in my line of sight and looking at me like I was some ghost. He did not take his eyes off me even for an instant. Like I would disappear if he blinked. At the exact moment Ronith honked and we both shook out of the daze.

"Come on, we are getting late.." He shouted.

I turned around and started walking towards the jeep

"What are you doing here?" He asked. It was more of a whisper than a question.

I turned around and looked at him. He was smiling and shaking his head in disbelief. I sat in the passenger seat and he climbed at the back.

"Ranjith, this is my cousin Veni. Veni…this is Ranjith, my childhood friend."

"Nice to meet you Veni." He said.

So his name was Ranjith. I repeated that in my head.

"It is nice to meet you too Ranjith."

We were all quiet for a couple of minutes as we drove towards the trek. Until Ronith decided to break the silence.

"So…Ranjith, how is it being a hot-shot Surgeon"?

I did a double take at him. He was a Surgeon? He was amused at my response and smiled.

"I am not a Surgeon yet but, it is not bad. Not entirely." And he smiled. I smiled politely. But it was not bad. It was good, very good indeed.

"So, what is your speciality Ranjith?" I asked him.

"I am an Orthopedic Doctor." He answered quietly.

"Oh wow. You are practicing right now on your own??"

"I am. I work with one Doctor. Deebak. He is my Professor in college. I assist him in his cases mostly."

I did a 180 degree turn and sat facing him in disbelief.

"You are not." I said in absolute disbelief.

He was confused. He look at me like he did not understand a word. Rohith announced just then

"We are here folks. Gather your gears. We are ready to conquer this peak."

We both smiled at his enthusiasm and climbed out of his jeep and took our bags. We started walking behind

Ronith as he explained to us that this is the smallest trek in the whole of Arunachal and yet is very scenic. All the other trek took 5-7 days at least to reach the peak.

We were mesmerised by the beauty of nature. The fresh air, the forest, the ferns and trees were all so surreal. It evoke a very pleasant feeling inside of me. I was starting to believe it was peace. I did not think of Krishna, the failed marriage, my parents. This moment was just me and how I felt one with this place.

"What did you mean back in the jeep?"

I heard Ranjith's voice from behind me. He jogged up and feel in step with me. I had to look up to see his face and that's when I realised the man was tall. And I have to crank up my neck to see him. My brain came back to focus again.

"What did you mean when you said that you don't believe it that I work with Dr. Deebak."

I had to take 10 seconds before I remembered it all again. I stopped to face him.

"The world is very small Dr. Ranjith." I smiled at him. He was still not sure where I was getting at.

"You are the same Ranjith Roy who has been sending emails about Ashwin's recovery to our office. It is just a coincidence that we meet? It is unbelievable."

"If you guys keep stopping like this and talking, we are going to miss the Sunrise. Come on." Ronith yelled from a few meters above.

I turned around and walked and Ranjith followed.

Ranjith

I walked behind her. There was something truly magical about this place. Perhaps not magic, but a place untouched by malice and hatred. The forest seemed so peaceful. The air was fresh and although it was cold, the trek was keeping us warm.

I looked ahead and saw Veni taking in the scenery. She was lost in this moment so much, she seemed like a painting. There was something about her that seemed familiar. The way she stood in front of meemaw's house and looked at it. It felt she belonged here.

She started to walk and I interrupted her and asked her what she meant. I was shocked when she said I was the one sending Ashwin's recovery update emails. Who was she? It did not strike me for a while. But I connected the dots. She went with Pragya the other day into her office. Was she Doctor Vishu's colleague? My mind went into an overdrive and she chose to turn around and walk. Ronith was asking us to walk faster since the sun would be up soon and we did not want to miss the sunrise.

Who was this woman. And why is she here?

We reached the top of the trek just in time. We caught our breath and stood there. The sun rose in all its glory. Turning the blue black sky to pinkish orange. It wouldn't be wrong to say that I felt that the darkness in my life was soon going to wane away. The loses I have faced, the battles I have fought are all meaningful. I stood there taking in the moment looking at the sky. I turned around and saw Veni. She was looking at the sky and in an instant turned and looked me in the eye. She smiled gently as if she understood and turned away. We stood there for a while and sat down.

"Oh man, I am exhausted." Ronith exclaimed.

"Any of you have any water?"

Veni handed over a bottle of water to him. We sat down on the hill top and looked at the world around us.

"You know, there is a temple in the hills here, it belongs to our ancestors." Ronith said.

"You guys want to take a look at it on the way down?"

"Sure. I don't mind" Veni responded.

I nodded as well.

We sat there for a few more minutes, Ronith got up and dusted his pants. We took it as our cue to leave as well. This day was peaceful. I desired nothing more at this point.

Hansa

Trekking downhill was easy. When Ronith asked us if we wanted to check out an old temple, I said yes. I have never been in touch with my roots. This is my ancestors and I was not going to pass up any chances of getting to know my lineage at all. We walked down the same path we trekked for a while. There was an intersection that lead towards denser wood. Ronith stopped and turned back. Ranjith was a few steps behind me.

"Ok...so, we go this way, the roads are narrow and walk closely. Don't have to worry about wild animals, just insects and snakes."

My heart just jumped to my throat.

"What!? Snakes??"

Both the men started to laugh. I realised he was just kidding. I hit his arm playfully.

"But I must tell you about this legend."

He turned back and looked at the both of us.

"Centuries back" and he continued walking. We followed closely.

"Our ancestors were attacked by enemies. Our ancestors were known for their healing abilities. No one could take over their village 'cos they were extremely powerful."

Ronith kept walking and we kept leaning into the story.

"But unfortunately, they were defeated and the secrets destroyed. But before they were all murdered. Our ancestors made a pact."

"What pact?" I asked. Ronith turned around and I saw a gleam in his eyes.

"A pact sealed with magic. The Moirang clan sealed a deal with magic that their blood, the descents of their clan who carry magic in their blood, and purity in their hearts; Will meet again. They will bring back the magic to the world again."

I got goosebumps listening to this. "is this real Ronith?"

"Its a legend Veni. I want to believe in it. I want to see it happen." He looked at me and Ranjith and I knew he knew something more.

We reached the temple of Siko Dido. It was hidden inside the forest like a gem. I saw bells hanging in the pergolas made out of bamboo. The bright red, yellow and green flags hung across from them and there was a small cave like structure. I could hear the sound of a waterfall. It was like music to my ears. This place felt so familiar. I soaked every ounce of it.

"Why is this place called a temple?"

Ranjith asked.

"Well, the Moirang sisters made a pact here. They placed a talisman here and cast a spell. Anyone who comes here. Finds this place calming."

"Wait, so…they cast a spell on a talisman and left it here? I asked surprised.

Ronith just smiled.

"What does Siko dido mean?" Ranjith who was looking at the valley asked.

"Medicinal water of snow" Ronith replied.

"Where is the talisman Ronith?" I asked. Ronith turned facing me this time.

"Veni, in 200 years, no one has been able to find it."

It was mind boggling to get to know so much about my own self, my ancestors in a span of 6 hours. I wanted to sit down and take a sip of water. I removed my shoes, put my bag down and sat down near the cave. I couldn't believe it, but I knew in my gut this was true. What if everything Pragya used to tell me was true? What if magic was real. What if my anxiety attacks were not anxiety attacks and a direction my ancestors were asking me to go towards. I opted to shut my brain for a while. I opened the water bottle, but one more question popped into my head.

"Ronith... do you know the names of the sisters who casted a spell here?" I took the sip of water.

Ronith smiled and I saw the same gleam I saw earlier.

"Of course I do." He said and smiled. I looked at him and shrugged. "so tell me" I said.

"Pragya and Hamsaveni." He kept looking at me.

I dropped the water bottle and it rolled off. Was what I hearing real? Did he just say what he said?

Is this some kind of joke? So many questions ran inside my head. Ronith looked at me, holding my eyes and looked at Ranjith. I turned my head and looked at him too.

Ranjith was clicking pictures of this place. Ronith's eyes met mine again. And I did not know what to make of it.

I got up and started to look for my water bottle that had rolled off. It was hiding behind one of the big rocks in a creek. I will have to crawl in and get the bottled out. I peeped in to see how deep this creek was, it was not deep and was lit with sunlight from the opposite side. I decided to crawl in and fetch my bottle.

I pulled my bottle out but it was stuck to something. A tiny rope like thing was stuck at the mouth of my water bottle. Damn it I will have to crawl closer now. I crawled in deeper and yanked the rope. The moment I touched it, it glowed and I immediately pulled my hand away. Was it a live wire? What if I get a shock? But something inside me urged to pull the rope. I took my bottle in one hand, it touched the ends of the rope and pulled it. It glowed but this time not like earlier, may be the sunlight went through the rocks.

It was a beautiful crystal bead chain. Dirty, with mud and rocks covered. I held it and crawled back out. The sun was out in full glory and my eyes had to readjust to the light.

"Where did you disappear?" Ranjith asked me. And he looked at the bead I was holding.

"Oh wow did you find that here?"

Ronith kept looking at me. I walked to him and showed him the bead and he just smiled. What does this mean? The bead glowed when I touched it. Is this the talisman.

"Veni can I see the bead please?" Ranjith asked from behind me. Ronith nodded and asked me to show him. I handed over the bead to Ranjith and the moment he touched it. The beads had a glow too. Ranjith's head whipped up to meet my eyes. His eyes went wide.

"Did you see that? Did you see the beads glow?"

I nodded and Ronith laughed. We were confused. Ranjith was equally confused too.

The clouds started to descend slowly. Ronith looked at the sky and signalled us.

"Let's go guys. Veni, put the beads in your bag. Put it in a cloth and then keep it inside. It might be delicate."

I took off my bandana and wrapped the beads inside and kept it inside my bag. We started the trek back to the jeep. My mind was racing with so many questions. Ronith knows a lot more than I can imagine and I have to pick his brains.

Ranjith

The view of the valley from here was more than heavenly. I couldn't stop thinking about my parents.

Did my mother come here when she was a young girl?. Ronith said most of our people knew about this...this place is a legend. I regretted not hearing about this from mom. I regretted not coming to spend summers with meemaw and that moment I realised how important it was to know who you are, where you come from. Science tells her that our existence contains 800 years of information in our DNA. Our evolution. I was lost in my thoughts when I heard Ronith chuckle. He was looking at Veni crawl into a creek.

"Where is she going man?" I asked him.

"She dropped her bottle and is going to get it."

When she returned, she was holding a bead of sorts in her hand. She had a puzzled look on her face and went straight to Ronith.

I went closer and asked her if I can see it. Veni let me hold the crystals. But when I touched them, they glowed. I was shocked and looked at Veni

"Did you see it glow?" They both nodded. Holy shit! This is unreal. May be what they say about Mayong is after all true. May be there is magic.

I looked at Veni. She was equally in awe of this. She was like magic herself. Seeing her here, meeting her. I looked at her and I saw a glow around her. I liked her the first time I met her and I have been wanting to get to know here ever since. Why would there be so many coincidences. Why would she walk into my life. My world and my whole existence if we were not meant to be. My mind went somewhere else for a second and I had to shake myself out of it.

Ronith asked us to trek down so we can go back home. I was famished and I could definitely use a good meal. As we walked down the rocky slippery road Veni slipped a step.

"Hold on to each other, the road is slippery with all the mist"

I extended my arm and Veni looked up at me. She held my hand and I felt a jolt and she shook for a second and looked at me. I knew she felt it too. There was definitely something magical about this place. We held each others hand for the rest of the trek downhill. I was not going to let go of her hand and neither did she. It felt surreal to walk hand in hand with her. With her walking in front of me and she occasionally glanced at me. There was something about this trek. I felt myself at peace.

Hamsa

We reached home by afternoon. Ronith and I dropped Ranjith off first. The way he looked at me when he got down from the jeep, the way he held my hand during the trek…it left me with a deep longing. A longing I never felt. I did not want him to leave. I looked at him as he walked into that house.

"Its beautiful." Ronith said looking at me.

"What's happening Ronith? What are you not telling me?"

"I already told you everything you need to know Veni. You just have to put the pieces together. It is upto you now."

What is upto me? Am I supposed to assume I am the descendent that will complete the legend? How am

I supposed to fulfil that destiny? Is it some sort of joke? Should ask Ronith all of this. So many things ran in my mind and yet I couldn't bring my mouth to utter a single word. By the time I could make sense of all of it... we reached home. Ronith dropped me and with a knowing smile he left.

I walked into my room and put my things down. My mom came looking for me and asked me how the trek was. I told her I visited the ancestral temple and she was beyond thrilled. She told me how she went there as an unmarried girl and it was the tradition. I was confused. What was tradition?

"The legend says that the chosen descendent of Moirang will find the beads of magic and that she will fulfil the destiny of our clan."

My jaw dropped to the floor. I was unable to come to terms with this information. My heart raced and I could hear it pounding in my chest. My mother was going on and on about how for over 100 years no one has found the beads and now it just seems like a legend and just that. In a second I wanted to tell her the truth but I know what fulfilling that destiny meant. I am supposed to find my man and marry him. The very thought of marriage shook my core and I decided to keep quiet for now. My mom asked me to get fresh and come and have lunch. I realised how hungry I was.

Once my mother left the room, I called Ronith.

He picked up the call.

"Why didn't you tell me Ronith.?" I practically yelled.

"I always knew it would be you Veni. I just wanted to prove it to myself."

"What…what are you talking about.?"

I could hear Ronith breathing.

"You remember why you stopped coming to the village?"

I remembered it. I came here when I was young. Every year. One fateful year, during the Siang festival I fell into the river. I drowned and that's all I remember and the fear of water set in from then.

"I remember Ronith. I remember you being there too."

"Do you remember who saved you?"

I had no clue how I came to the shores. I was opened my eyes and I saw my parents and friends. They were looming over me and I remember the worried faces.

"I don't."

"When you drowned that day. I was there. I was on the other side of the river and was shouting at the top of my voice for help. And a miracle happened. A wave carried you to the shore and gently placed you there. I thought I was dreaming. May be some sort of trauma. But more I have spent my time here in the valley, the more I believe that magic is here. And you are the chosen one."

It all came back rushing like a sudden wave to me. The fear, the drowning, the running into the forests, the blooming flowers.

"If I had told you Veni, you wouldn't have believed. Now you know. And you will know what to do."

I kept quiet all the while. Ronith cut the call I stood there holding on to the phone. Stuck between who I was a week back. A physio who was a realist and now just a tribal girl who believes in magic. I wanted to go back to the real world. My real world where I don't have to question the purpose of my existence. I would go back to being an ace Physio. Tomorrow, I will go to the Siang festival with my folks and then I leave. One more day. One more day. I kept telling myself.

Ranjith

I remember just walking back home. My feet wouldn't move but I dragged myself out of the jeep and walked home. I remember only coming back and lying down. I wake up and its morning. Holy cow! I had slept like the dead and no one bothered to wake me up. My stomach growled angrily and I realised I had slept for more than 12 hours. My mama walked into the room with a glass of juice. I plucked it out of his hand and drank the entire glass of juice in one single gulp. He laughed a hearty laugh.

"Breakfast is ready. But make haste, we have to leave for the festival. You don't wanna miss it."

I jumped out of bed and got ready in about 15 seconds. I went into the dining room, served myself generously with the breakfast and whiffed it off in minutes. Mama was already outside with his baskets of fruits and offerings for the festival. I dressed up in a kurta for the festival.

We reached the banks of Siang. The entire community was already there. Some familiar faces, some unfamiliar. Some older women held my face and kissed my forehead. They were as old as my Meemaw. I sat down with a few of them, telling tales of their times with meemaw, their memories of her and my mother. They knew so much about their life. The life I knew nothing about and that's what is beautiful. My family was not just my family. They belonged to this community too and I realised I had received so much in the past few days. These memories won't fade at all.

Just as I was getting ready to leave I spotted Veni. She was with her parents and was paying her respects to the elders of the tribe. One of the older women hugged her and put a hand on her head and blessed her. Veni closed her eyes for a brief moment and something crossed her face. Like she was sad. She opened her eyes and smiled at the elders and went her way. I kept looking at her and she turned to look at me and her eyes went wide for a second and then she smiled. I smiled back.

I paid my respects to the river and came and settled down under a banyan tree.

"I keep seeing you like this, makes me believe its not a coincidence anymore"

I smiled knowing it is Veni's voice. I turn around and look at her.

"That's very accurate."

We both laugh and she comes and sits next to me.

I wanted to ask her so many things. But at that moment I couldn't speak at all. I finally managed to speak.

"Veni, I never got to thank you for saving Rakesh's life. Thank you. I don't know what would have happened if you had not been there that day."

"It is ok Ranjith. Any decent human being would have done that."

"Any decent human being wouldn't have paid admission fees for strangers and left without providing a contact number."

She laughed. A hearty laugh that had sincerity filled in it.

"You saved my life. Consider the debt paid."

She looked at me and I could see she was grateful. And I accepted that and nodded my head. Cannot argue with a woman who is sincere and truthful.

She asked me about my parents, my meemaw. I told her about them, their demise. My struggle through college. How Rakesh was family and why it had meant so much to me. She told me about her parents, her mother's family belonging here and her summer holidays at the village. Her ties with her family. I felt a pang of jealousy but it overcame with a warm feeling of knowing she has that family to love her. And I felt glad that I got to experience the love of my parents too.

Veni's phone rang and it was her mother.

"I am sorry I have to leave. I will see you soon." And then she disappeared before I could ask her for her number. I felt a strange connection with her and I know she felt it too. I was about to leave when I overheard a conversation where Veni was mentioned.

I got curious and walked close enough to eves drop. Two women were talking about Veni and her family. How she was saved from drowning and then never came back for a long time. I felt sorry for her.

"I am so glad she is getting married. She has always listened to her parents."

I felt a dagger through my heart. She was getting married? Veni was getting married! She never mentioned it. I felt a range of emotions in one second. Anger, rage, betrayal. Those emotions hit me like a truck and I couldn't stay there anymore. Why hadn't Veni mentioned getting married. She pretended to like me. Was she just leading me on?

I also felt stupid for thinking that she liked me. I walked home with all of these in my mind. I had to pack my things. I have a flight tomorrow and I need to get everything in order. My mind first.

Hamsa

It has been a week since we came back from Mayong. My mother was happy and content. My father and I enjoyed this happy "her" while it lasted. Work was keeping my life busy. Pragya had taken all of my patients for the week I wasn't here and she was so relieved that I was back. She hugged me and asked me never to leave her again like this with my patients. I laughed at her being so dramatic.

We both spoke about how some patients were adamant and would do exactly opposite of what we ask them to, over a cup of coffee. I met Vishnu sir and got an update on Ashwin. He was getting stronger and kept doing what was told.

Vishnu sir told me that Ashwin's parents had invited us to his birthday party and they have specifically asked me to be present. I couldn't refuse since Vishnu sir had been extremely understanding and I accepted the invite. I went back and checked on the progress emails. There were a few emails from Dr. Ranjith Roy. I wondered how he was doing.

We had a wonderful conversation back home. He spoke about his family, his roots where he came from. It was heartbreaking to know he had lost his parents. Him facing this world alone made me want to hold him. His sincerity towards his work. There was something about him that made me like him. He was real. Un-ashamed to show his emotions, show me how vulnerable he was at that moment. He trusted me and it was an honour. I smiled at the memory.

I had to pay a visit to Ashwin who was getting discharged in a couple of days. I had a session in a few hours. I packed my bag, informed the office about my appointment and left for the session. Ashwin was happy to see me and asked me about my trip. We worked out together and slowly told him about the trip. He was thrilled to hear the details and told me, once he gets better, he will definitely visit northeast and explore the beauty. He reminded me about his birthday and told me strictly to be present. I laughed at his mock strictness and gave him a salute. We were done with our session and I gave Ashwin some pointers and left the building.

I walked to the parking lot. I had got my car today 'cos seemed like it would rain. The dark clouds were looming and a slow breeze kept the climate cold enough to feel the goosebumps.

As I approached my car, I saw Krishna leaning against my car. With his hands crossed and looking down. The moment he saw me coming he stood upright and smiled. I had ignored his calls and messages ever since we parted ways and I had blocked him too. I just wanted privacy while I processed the grief. But now, looking at him I had no grief at all. I was glad he did the right thing no matter how hard it had been on me, on us. He had the courage to do it.

I smiled at him as I approached the car.

"I never thought you would smile at me again"

Krishna said. I laughed at the statement.

"I thought so too. But turns out, I can't hold grudges. Especially with people I loved."

Krishna's eyes became sad. I could see the regret in his eyes. He held my hand.

"I am sorry Veni. I know I was an ass. I don't have an explanation…justification at all. Please try to forgive me."

I held on to his hand and nodded.

"I forgive you… but only at one condition."

Krishna looked at me in surprise.

"You will have to name your first born after me."

He was mortified and I laughed.

"I am just kidding. Please don't do that."

He laughed and he gently hugged me. In that embrace I felt affection and admiration and I knew I have earned a friend for life. We let each other go and I promised him I would unblock him so he could invite me to his wedding.

I would have never, in a million years imagined to have gotten here, to get over a broken engagement and become friends with the ex-fiancee had I not met Ranjith.

I had not felt something so powerful with anyone. His presence calmed me. And talking to him was easy. I just smiled and was about to get into the car when another car pulled up next to my parking spot. I was about to walk into the drivers side when I saw Ranjith get down from the car. I was overjoyed. This is crazy. I just thought of him and he was here.

"Should I call it stalking 'cos its one too many times to be a coincidence."

Ranjith looked at me and did not smile. There was something odd in the way he looked at me. He was wearing dark glasses. I couldn't figure out what he was thinking. He was aloof. Not the man I met in the mountains. I took a step back to understand if I had offended him in anyway. He took off his glasses and I could see disgust. And just as when I completed that thought in my head.

And just like that he walked away. I stood there not understand what just happened. Tears flowed down my eyes and at the exact same moment it started to rain. Why did Ranjith just insult me? Why am I putting myself in the path of men who just stomp on my heart and walk away. I held myself together and sat in the car and drove away. Never again I thought to myself.

RANJITH

I had a review with Ashwin today. Dr. Deebak had asked me to come and meet with him and discuss Ashwin's discharge as well. I drove into the parking lot and the dagger lodged in my heart dug only deeper. There was not one moment when I had not thought of Veni in the last week and she was here, in the parking lot, laughing and smiling with someone. A man I remember seeing somewhere and I had met him too. He asked me how do I say "I love you" in Bengali; and he was holding Veni's hand and they were looking at each other.

I felt hurt and betrayed all over again and that moment she chose to hug him. Like an embrace that meant something. I did not want to interrupt their little moment so I decided I would park somewhere else and drove on. All the other spots were full and I had to take a full turn and come back to where she had parked her car. I had no option. I got down from the car. Veni saw me and came rushing towards me. All my feelings for her came rushing too. It felt like I became an entirely different person at that point. I remember her asking me something and instead of speaking to her like an adult, I threw a temper tantrum. I vaguely remember and walking away giving her a look of disgust.

My ego got bigger than the person I was. I saw the hurt in her eyes and it broke my heart. I know what I had done was irreversible. I kept walking away without looking back and I knew I was wrong.

I walked into Ashwin's room before I could see Dr. Deebak. Just wanted to catch up with the guy and see how he was doing. Ashwin was just done with his physiotherapy session and was settling down.

" Hey Man…long time no see." Ashwin called out.

I walked close to him and gave him a casual hug.

"Indeed man. You are looking good. Been on track huh?"

Ashwin laughed. "yeah yeah. You know my Therapist, Won't take no for an answer."

"Hans was here?" I asked

"Yep. Just left moments before you walked in." And with that he settled down on his bed and turned-on the

TV. Must have missed him walking out. I was about to leave when Ashwin called out.

"Hey Doc! My parents are throwing a birthday party for me. I want you there. Will leave the details in the office for you. No excuses." And he winked at me. I laughed at his expression. This kid has grown on me.

"I won't miss it for the world." And Ashwin just shook his head in disbelief. I walked out to Dr. Deebak's office.

"So…how is my fav student doing?" He came in for an embrace. "I am sorry about your grandmother Ranjith." And he stepped back. Looking at me and gestured me to sit down.

"Thank you Doctor Deebak. I guess she lived a full life and I am glad I got to say goodbye to her" Dr. Deebak Just nodded.

"How is Ashwin doing? He is looking good." I told Doctor Deebak.

"Yeah. His Physio has been bending him backwards to get back up on his feet and the boy listens." He chuckled.

"Hans is the Physio right?"

"Yes. The magicians Hans." And he laughed. "you will get to meet Vishnu's magician at Ashwin's birthday party. It is an official invite from his family. Try not to skip it."

Great, I will finally get to meet the magician I have heard so much about him. I was definitely looking forward to it. Dr. Deebak discussed multiple cases with me and we discussed in detail about the surgeries our schedules and so on.

The schedule seemed packed for the coming weeks. With my application in colleges. With working under Dr.

Deebak, the prep I had to do before assisting the Doctor. All of this was going to keep me busy and I was happy being that way.

Hansa

The worst thing about grief is that no matter how hard you push it to the corner of your mind, it finds its way back. In the most unexpected times. The grief needs to be addressed. Grief needs to be processed. The truth is, I did not even know I was grieving. The loss of something I never really had was unacceptable and yet, looking at Ranjith walk into a room full of strangers was somehow the highlight of my week. I know I made a promise to myself that I wouldn't put myself in the path of men who wouldn't value me but, looking at him walk into the room made my resolve weaker. I wanted to go and talk to him and ask him what was wrong. My pride got in the way and pushed me to walk away from him.

Pragya was with me and noticed me walking away and followed me.

"Are you alright Veni?

You've been so lost for the last couple of weeks. Is everything ok?"

I just turned around and looked at her. I smiled at her and nodded my head. Ashwin's parents were really loaded. Wealthy entrepreneurs. The house was expansive to say the least. Pragya and I had walked into the lawn and the party was inside the house. We sat down in silence and looked into the room where people were socialising, singing and laughing. We sat in the lawn bench; in silence.

Pragya looked at me as if she wanted to ask something. But she held her words back. Turned away from me and looked at all the people inside the room.

"Sometimes, all we need is the attention from that one person Veni. One person who has the power to make or break us. Their mood decides our mood. Their happiness is everything for us. Finding that one person is the most difficult thing in the world."

I turn my head and look at her. She was still looking straight.

"Geez Prags, you have become a philosopher."

She laughed and slapped my arm playfully.

"Let's go inside. I don't want to miss the cake."

Pragya got up and straightened her clothes and motioned me to walk with her. I got up reluctantly from the bench and we walked back inside.

As we opened the door and went inside, my eyes found Ranjith's eyes. He wouldn't look away, he held my gaze and I held his. I gave nothing away. This man knew nothing about me and for some reason thought was better than me. I reminded myself that he is just an overgrown man child who needs to learn to communicate. Him looking at me is not going to get him an apology. I finally looked away as Pragya and I joined Vishnu sir and our other colleagues who were sitting together and discussing each others life choices.

I joined them and I was going to be roasted for sure. My colleagues started the assault. I got roasted for being at office all the time, for being a hard ass on my celebrity patients. It felt good to speak about all the old times. I realised how much work I had put in to be where I am today. So many hours spent at work. Working with patients, reading about new techniques everyday and applying them at work.

The gang was rowdy and bustling with laughter when Dr. Deebak walked upto our group. His minions followed and I noticed Ranjith joining us too. It made me mildly uncomfortable but I wasn't going to walk away. I own this group. This is my circle and I am not walking away because some wannabe surgeon decided to piss on my pride. I stood there and faced Dr. Deebak and he smiled at me.

He caught up with Vishnu sir and they had their own banter. Just when I was about to step aside Dr. Deebak decided to talk to me. Ranjith was right behind him and he was focussed on me.

"Hans. How are you doing?"

"I am fine Doctor! How are you?"

"You know, the usual. Cutting open patients and putting them back…" we both chuckled.

"Well I am glad you are putting them back together properly. Else making them work would be difficult. You are good and I am glad…"

Dr. Deebak and I both laughed and suddenly he turned…

"Hey Ranjith come here…" and my heart lodged in my throat for a second. What was happening.

"Dr. Ranjith…this is our Magician Hans. Hamsaveni. Ace physiotherapist and Orthopaedic occupational therapist. I can go on and on about her specialty but, to make it short and sweet, she is the best of the best we have got."

Ranjith's eyes went as wide as they could. He was not expecting me to be something, let alone an ace physio with sports rehabilitation as a speciality. I am sure his male ego pegged me to be some chick trying to get her life together. My chest was swollen with pride cos I felt victory at that moment. But Dr.Deebak continued.

"Ranjith wanted to get an introduction forever. He had been behind me for months. And Hans, Dr. Ranjith is a very talented Surgeon. You should look out for him."

I just smiled and was polite and nodded my head. Ranjith was dumb stuck. He did not know what to say and I excused myself, turned around and walked away from him at that moment towards Pragya. I could feel his eyes bore into the back of my head.

Pragya was shocked to see Ranjith and wanted to go and speak to him. Just then Ashwin showed up and it was time for cake. I could see Ranjith looking at me from the crowd. He never looked away not even for a moment. I did not want to look at him. It felt like he was calling out to me, begging me to look at him once so he could walk upto me. But I was done giving any man the right to put a dent in my armour. Especially this one who seemed special. I am not going to fall into the same pit of misery and self loathing again.

Ranjith

Dr. Deebak had specifically told me to make an attendance today. And I did. But from the time I have walked into this house, I feel a strange pull and I feel someone's been watching me. And at that exact moment Veni walked through the door. I couldn't take my eyes off her. My brain was asking me to look away but It seemed like I had no control over my coherence. She looked at me, held my gaze. But it was nothing like how we met before. A perfect stranger, and that broke my heart a little. What have I done? I thought to myself. My ego got the better of me and I have to find a way to apologise to Veni. But before any of that I wanted to meet Hans. I walked upto Dr. Deebak and asked him if he has seen Hans. And I would like to meet him.

"Oh yeah. I see Vishnu, Hans must be there too…" and he walked towards a gang of people who were laughing and talking animatedly. I spotted Veni there too. I knew she saw me. Dr. Deebak and Mr. Vishnu were old friends who have been working together for a few decades now. They bantered amongst themselves. Suddenly Dr. Deebak called out to Hans and I looked everywhere.

I was dumbstruck and realised it was Veni. Her full name was Hamsaveni. She was the one being referred to as the magician. How did I miss this. I felt really stupid for not being able to connect the dots. Dr. Deebak went on and on about her accomplishments and I could just stand there and look at her. Dr. Deebak introduced me to her and before I could say anything, she just turned around and walked away. Just like that. The cake was out and everyone gravitated towards the birthday boy and wished him.

I stood in the corner of the room, laughing at the enthusiasm of this boy. I stood there crossing my arm when Pragya appeared from nowhere.

"What did you do to piss off Veni?"

I turned and looked at her.

"Hello to you too…"

She just gave me a death glare and I raised my hands in surrender. And told her how we met, we spoke, how it felt like she was everything I ever wanted in life and as stupid as it might sound, I had fallen in love with her. But she played me, knowing very well that I liked her and she was going to go and marry someone else anyway. I told Pragya how betrayed I felt.

Pragya stood there arms crossed, head tilted sideways and she had tears in her eyes. She cleared her throat… I was waiting for her to hurl abuses at me

"You remember the day you saved her life?"

I nodded.

"Her fiancé Krishna… he had broken up with her."

I felt like a slap landed on my face. I realised why Veni wouldn't even look at me. In that moment I realised I had judged her too harshly. I did not bother asking her anything. Her life, what she did, what happened the other day. I was so absorbed in my life and how I felt, I ignored the fact that she had a life and she felt and saw things that I would never understand.

Pragya saw the regret and confusion on my face…

"Veni is extremely stubborn Ranjith… if she had made up her mind, it's gonna take a lot of effort for you to change it."

With that she turned and walked away and joined the crowd. I saw Veni give her a look. She just shrugged and they both went towards the Buffet to pick up their plates.

I stood there realising two things. I was in love with this woman and I had screwed it up big time. I have to suck it up, swallow my pride and surrender. This was not going to be easy but I figured this will be worth it.

The birthday party was well organised. I met Dr. Vishnu's team. A bunch of young and talented Physio's. Most of them practicing under Dr. Hamasaveni. They respected her know how, dedication and how she guided them to improve and better their skills as a physio. She was Dr. Vishnu's most trusted student. I also learnt that she was recruited fresh out of college and trained by Dr. Vishnu herself cos he saw the potential and drive in her. And it was Dr. Vishnu's mother who gave her the name magician 'cos she made her walk again after 5 years of being bed ridden. I realised one more thing. Hamsaveni is not just an extraordinary therapist, she was an amazing human being too and in that second I felt disgusted with myself to have judged her so soon and spit venom like that. I excused myself and went to look for her. She was talking to Ashwin's parents and was near the main door. Before I could call her, she stepped out of the main door and got in her car and left. I ran there just to see her car drive away. I knew how to get her to forgive me.

Hamsa

Ashwin's birthday was a good way to wind down from all the work stress and relax. The only flip to it was meeting Ranjith. I saw Pragya speaking to Ranjith in the party. I asked her what they spoke and she said they exchanged pleasantries and nothing else.

It was almost mid of the week. Pragya was constantly asking me why was I so weird to Ranjith. I wanted to tell her everything. How I felt about him, how much it scared me, what he said and how he judged me and I don't even know for what. But I decided I was going to just let it be and focus on my life. Life that I had built with so much focus and precision and that's what is going to save me.

I informed the office of my appointments. I had a few patients to meet in the Hospital. Dr. Deebak's team had assigned few complicated cases to our office and its me this week and I had to go and check them out before I worked out the schedule for everyone. The last thing I expected today was sitting face to face with Dr. Ranjith and getting the brief.

I was taken by surprise when he walked into the room and sat across from me and greeted me. What game was he playing. He did not apologise. He was being charming and acted like I had his complete attention. I took the brief from him, took all the files and walked in on each patient and met them. I had to focus and it was becoming difficult to focus with this man walking beside me.

Once I finished meeting all the patients. I bid adieu to the Doctors and walked out to the parking lot. I saw Ranjith waiting exactly at the spot krishna was and I just let out a heavy sigh. Why does this keep happening with me. I walked towards my car and Ranjith looked me in the eye. I did not smile. I kept looking at him and walked towards the car and unlocked it.

"Aren't you going to ask me what I am doing here?" He asked.

"It's none of my business Doctor."

He looked at the ground and took a deep breath.

"Veni… I am sorry. I was an absolute ass with you." He looked me in the eye. I crossed my arms and leaned on my car. I wanted to know why he insulted me…and what did I of to piss him off so much.

"I…" he hesitated… "when you left from Mayong, we had a conversation…under the banyan tree." He looked at me expectantly.

"Once you left I over heard a few women speak about your marriage. I was furious. You were so nice to me. I felt something between us. And I felt so betrayed, that you were marrying someone else."

I did not understand where this was going…and stood up a little straight.

"And when I saw you here… the other day, with that guy. I lost my sanity. I felt Anger and rage and I did not know how to control my emotions."

He looked me in the eye and I saw sincerity there. I could see the pain and all I wanted to do was let go of this stupid pride and tell him it was ok.

"I fell in love with you Veni. The day I met you. I felt complete. There was a huge hollow in my heart and that day, when I pulled you out of the road and onto me. I seemed to have filled that hollow with your presence. I am sorry I hurt you. I don't know what else to say but the truth…"

I don't know what took over me at that point, I walked into his arms and pulled him in for a kiss.

Ranjith was taken aback but in one second he jumped into that kiss. He pulled me closer and in that moment I lost myself entirely. It felt like a dream but I was there with

Ranjith. At the temple of Siko Dido. We both stood in front of the cave. I was wearing a traditional Moirang mekhla chador, a half sari of sorts and Ranjith was in his Gamcha, a dhoti. We stood there. There was rumbling thunder and we held the beads together in our hands and it started to glow. We looked into each others eyes and thunder plundered the sky. We both jumped and moved away from each other. We are in the parking lot.

Ranjith was panting and he looked confused and so was I.

"Did you see what I saw?" He asked me.

"Where we at Siko Dido?"

He nodded.

"We held the beads. It was glowing....you were wearing a Mekhla chador..."

We stood there... confused. We kissed for the first time and it was literally out of this world. Were we meant to be? Is he the man who is to fulfil the destiny along with me? Ranjith and I are going to be the legend that our clan so strongly believes in? So many things ran in my mind. So many questions. I was lost and panicking.

Ranjith stood there looking at me. Like he longed to hold me. And I felt that too but right now, I needed clarity, I needed to think what I was feeling, what I was imagining is not just hormonal. There has to be an explanation to it.

I tried to walk away but Ranjith blocked my way and looked me in the eye.

"Tell me you felt what I felt. And we will figure it out together."

I nodded my head. I told him what Ronith had told me the other day, during the trek. How my mother told me about the legend and me having found the beads. On top of it kissing this man had taken me to a parallel universe. We both just stood there, trying to make sense out of it and suddenly my phone started ringing... Ronith was calling me. It was a strange coincidence. I picked the call...

"Hello..."

"Veni... its Ronith."

"Yes Ronith...what a surprise."

"I am sure you know it's not... are you with Ranjith right now.?"

My eyes went wide and Ranjith got curious....

"Put me on speaker... I want to talk to the both of you."

I obeyed him and did so.

"Veni...Ranjith... I am sure you both would have figured out that something is not normal when it comes to the both of you. You both are not just regular human beings. You are here for a purpose and its time now. I want the both of you to come to Mayong as soon as possible.. and Bring Pragya with you."

With that he cut the call. We looked at each other. Neither of us had any idea about what Ronith was speaking about. And how did he know about Pragya. But with what we felt...Ranjith and I. We knew we had to know the whole truth.

The travel begins....

www.ingramcontent.com/pod-product-compliance
Lightning Source LLC
La Vergne TN
LVHW041131150826
845673LV00007B/2270

* 9 7 9 8 8 8 9 0 9 8 9 7 3 *